SamanthaSaurus
REX

by B. B. MANDELL

Illustrated by SUZANNE KAUFMAN

BALZER + BRAY
An imprint of HarperCollins *Publishers*

They say that when a baby hatches . . .
she comes out exactly the way she'll be her whole
life. Samanthasaurus Rex was no exception.

Most T. rexes liked to chase animals.
Samanthasaurus liked to paint them.

Most T. rexes liked to gnaw bones.
Samanthasaurus liked to sort them.

Most T. rexes liked to bite and fight.
Samanthasaurus liked to use her words.

"Girls need to be strong," said her mother.

"I can be strong," said Samanthasaurus.

"Girls need to be leaders," said her father.

"I can be a leader," said Samanthasaurus.

"Girls need to make a lot of NOISE!" said her big brother.

"Oh, I can definitely do THAT!" said Samanthasaurus.

One swampy morning, Samanthasaurus and her family went on a hike up Mount Crushmore.

"Come help me whack these branches," said her mother. But Samanthasaurus had found a grove of prehistoric ferns.

"If I weave these together," said Samanthasaurus, "they'll make a rope!"

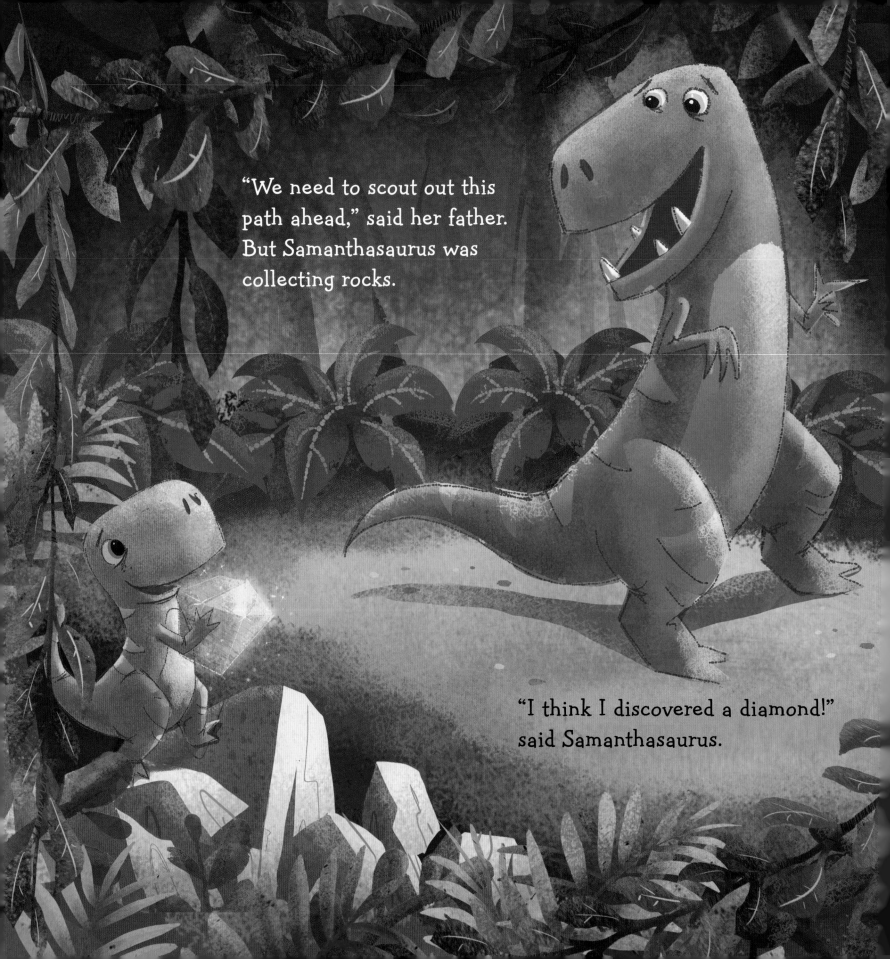

"We need to scout out this path ahead," said her father. But Samanthasaurus was collecting rocks.

"I think I discovered a diamond!" said Samanthasaurus.

"Let's stomp out those geysers,"
said her little brother.

"Let's *harness* that energy,"
said Samanthasaurus.

Her family climbed ahead.
Samanthasaurus was tired after
all her thinking.

As she relaxed in a hot spring,
she looked up at the sky. "It's
getting awfully dark," she said.

She saw a flock of pteranodons
speed past her overhead. "Why
are they flying so fast?" she
wondered.

She smelled something smoky in the air. "Hmm. Rotten stegosaurus eggs . . . or maybe not?" she said.

Something was up. Samanthasaurus lay quiet and still.

That's how she heard a rumble.
The mountain began to shake.
The trees began to sway.
And her hot bath got hotter.

"This isn't just an ordinary mountain!" said Samanthasaurus. She looked for her family. They were climbing higher and higher.

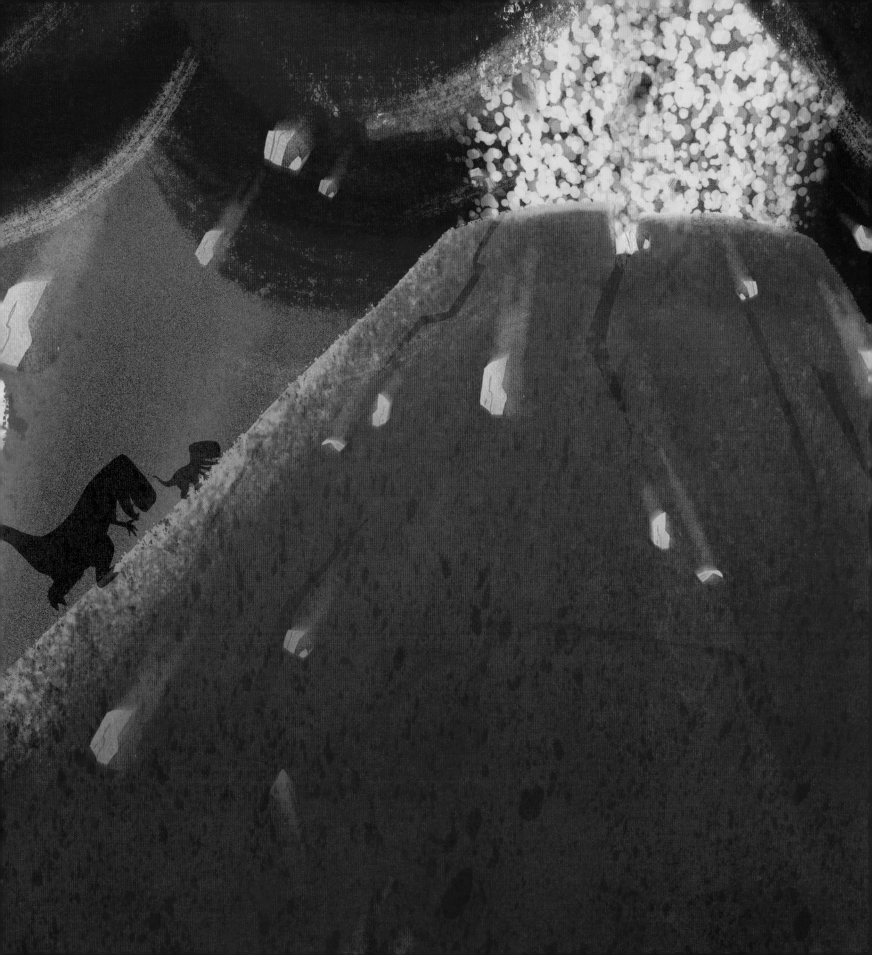

A massive rock fell on her mother's tail. Her mother could not reach it with her tiny arms.

"I'll help you, Mama!" said Samanthasaurus.

Samanthasaurus grabbed her fern rope and raced up the mountain. She tied one end to the rock and used all her strength to pull hard on the other.

Then Samanthasaurus looked up the trail and saw her father. He didn't notice he was about to be swept up into a river of lava.

"I'll save you, Papa!" said Samanthasaurus.

Samanthasaurus whipped out her diamond rock and used the sun's reflection to light up a path through the smoke.

Her father followed her path
out of the way of the lava.
Papa was out of danger!

Next, a big mudslide came in between
Samanthasaurus and her brother.

Samanthasaurus
ROARED!

She made so much noise that the pteranodons returned. They swooped down and plucked Samanthasaurus and her brother out of a hot mess.

Samanthasaurus helped her family get all the way down the mountain.

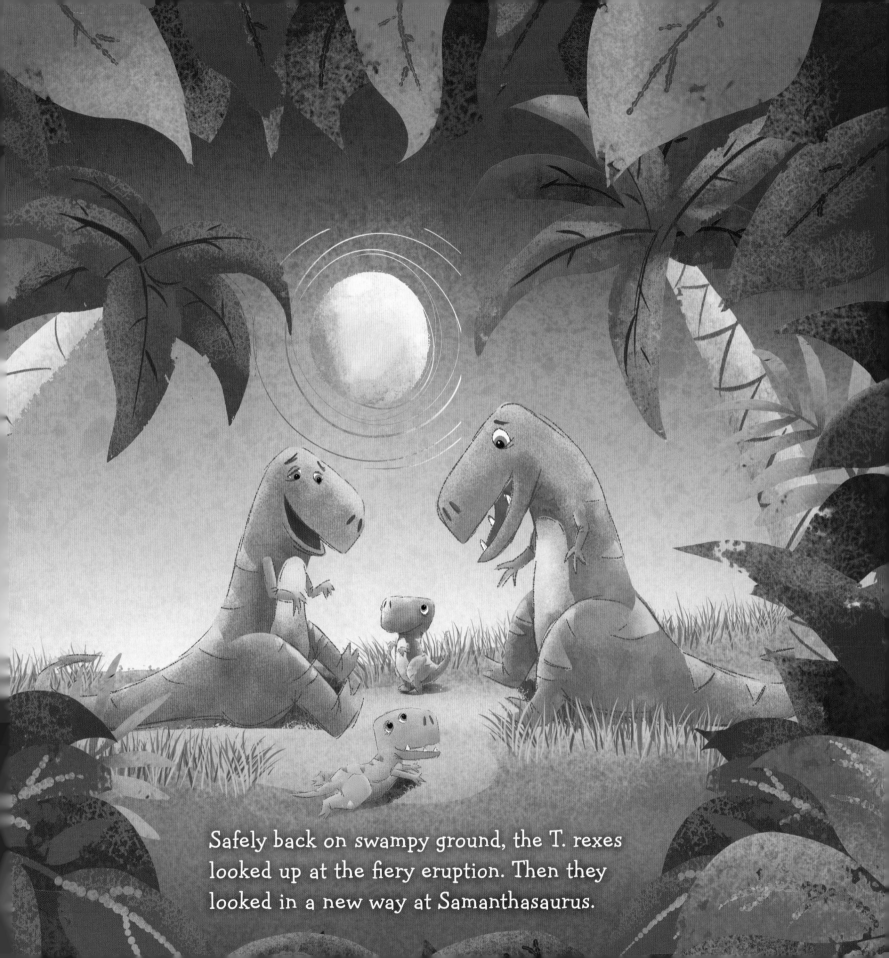

Safely back on swampy ground, the T. rexes
looked up at the fiery eruption. Then they
looked in a new way at Samanthasaurus.

"You are strong," said her mother.

"I got that from you," said Samanthasaurus.

"You are a leader," said her father.

"I know my way around," said Samanthasaurus.

"You made a lot of noise," said her brother.

"*Roar*," said Samanthasaurus quietly.

She looked up at her family.
"One more thing," she said.
"I didn't finish my bath.
Want to join me?"

The T. rexes hugged Samanthasaurus with their tiny arms.

"Oh yes," they said, "we can definitely do that."

For Charlie and Harry —B.B.M.

For all the mighty girls in the world,
and for my mom and big sis, Merrie —S.K.

Balzer + Bray is an imprint of HarperCollins Publishers.

Samanthasaurus Rex. Text copyright © 2016 by B. B. Mandell. Illustrations copyright © 2016 by Suzanne Kaufman. All rights reserved. Manufactured in China. No part of this book may be used or reproduced in any manner whatsoever without written permission except in the case of brief quotations embodied in critical articles and reviews. For information address HarperCollins Children's Books, a division of HarperCollins Publishers, 195 Broadway, New York, NY 10007. www.harpercollinschildrens.com

ISBN 978-0-06-234873-9 (trade bdg.)

The artist used pencil, ink, watercolor and Photoshop to create the illustrations for this book. Typography by Ellice M. Lee
16 17 18 19 20 SCP 10 9 8 7 6 5 4 3 2 1
❖
First Edition